Kira's Little Princess

An MDLG and ABDL lesbian story of a backpacker hostel event manager and how she convinced her baby girl to stay

By Tina Moore

Table of Contents

Chapter 1

"Thank you for flying with us. Enjoy your trip, and if you are coming home welcome home," the pilot said over the speaker. I was happy to be landing it had been a terrible flight. I had thought that getting the window seat would be great and it had been until I needed to use the bathroom in the middle of the night. I had to carefully climb over the two people sitting next to me to get to the aisle. I was happy I hadn't stepped on them. I had tried to get some sleep, but the plane had flown through turbulence most of the way, and the smell of the plane food had made me feel sick. I looked out the window and was surprised how big the airport was, I hadn't traveled very much and had just assumed everywhere expect my home town as well, less than. But the size of the terminals here rivaled any at home, and I followed the signs sleepily until I reached the one I was looking for.

"Hi, I'm Sasha, do you guys go to the Waker's Beach hostel?" I asked a tanned blonde. The woman was more excited than I was ready for and almost blew me away with her enthusiasm.

"We sure do! I'm Kira, I'm the events co-coordinator at the hostel and today, the taxi, how long are you going to stay with us, we have some great things planned this week," Kira said ticking my name off the clipboard and writing something down. I looked at her with tired eyes. I smiled at Kira and went to find a spot to sit while I waited for the other people to be ticked off Kira's clipboard list. Watching Kira, I wondered how long she had been at the hostel to be given the job. I liked how friendly she was. Her big smile and brown eyes had been so welcoming and warm. It made me feel less alone. I had originally planned the trip with my best friend Georgia, but she had bailed last minute. We had even made it the airport before Georgia had started having a panic attack just as we were going through customs. She had to be escorted out. It was pretty embarrassing.

I had already gone through and was waiting for her on the other side when I heard them say they would have to take her away. Georgia had yelled that I could still go, and if it hadn't been for Georgia's repeat offending with this type of stuff, maybe I wouldn't be here at all. It wasn't the first time Georgia had let me down like this, and I had felt so fed up with her on and off again way of being, I had decided to go on without her.

"Alright, everyone, on the bus," Kira called, breaking me out of the sleep I hadn't realized I was in. Laughing, Kira came up to me.

"It's OK sleepy head. Once we get to the hostel you can sleep all day. I know the flight is rough!" Kira said taking one of my bags and walking with me to the bus. Kira started talking to me about how she had planned to take everyone sand dune tobogganing and to watch the turtles hatch on the beach over the course of next week, but I hardly heard a word.

When I was finally on the shuttle bus, I put in my earphones and listened to the songs Georgia and I had put into a playlist and wondered how she was. No, fuck her, I thought, being angry that Georgia had let me down once again. The bus seemed to drive for forever, and Kira would stand up and talk on the microphone when we were passing something important or exciting. I liked her voice. It was full of excitement and playfulness. I imaged that Kira would be the first person on the dance floor at a party twirling and giggling as she let the music take over her. Going through the city, I looked out the window on the other side to see people walking down the street wearing fancy business suits and dresses and smiled to myself thinking about the life I had left behind.

I had worked for a photography company, and while I never wore such high-end fashion, I took pictures of the types of people who did. I would go into their homes, take their photo with their picture-perfect families and purebred dogs. Trying to capture something other than the fake happiness they were all trying so desperately to portray. Once or twice, I had ended up fucking the maid or the au pair in the main bedroom or outside on the balcony. I had wondered why I could never refuse them but knew deep in my heart it was because I just wanted the thrill. My job was easy, almost too easy and I liked the idea of getting fired and having to find something else to do with my time.

The bus came to a screeching halt, pushing me forward and then back against my seat, making me wondered if the driver had done that on purpose or not.

"Alright, everyone, welcome to your new home!" Kira said opening the door as people started to leave the bus. For the first time, I noticed that I was slightly older than most of the people who had been on the bus, watching them as they dismounted. At only 25, I hadn't felt very old, but listening to the conversations of the kids, on the bus, I felt like I had my life together way more than they did. I saw the typical 18-year-olds excitedly drinking cheap wine as they walked past me, offering me some.

"No, I'm good," I just replied. It's 10 in the morning, you bloody moron. I thought as I looked behind me to realize I was the last on the bus.

"Come on, sleepyhead," Kira said kindly doing one last sweep of the bus. She waited for me to get up and follow her out of the bus.

"Hey, you forgot this," Kira said holding up a photo of a girl that had fallen out of my pocket. Kira looked at me questioningly.

"Girlfriend?" She asked, her sparkling eyes making me look down, feeling stupid for what I was about to say.

"You'll think I'm dumb. She's my ex, this trip was to get over her," I said getting embarrassed. Kira thought for a minute before grabbing the photo from my hands.

"Well, you won't get over her by having her around. I'll hold onto it, and if you're still hooked by the time you leave, I'll give it back to you," Kira said. Usually, I would have grabbed the photo back, but I liked how nice Kira was and could tell she wasn't trying to be mean, so I just nodded and looked to the floor as I got off the bus.

"You'll be alright. Good girl for listening to me," Kira said as she passed me my bags from under the bus. I held my breath, making Kira laugh as I registered the words Kira had just said. Giving me a mischievous smile, Kira tapped the side of the bus, and it drove off in a plume of smoke. Waiting for the dust to settle, I turned and looked at the hostel.

"Come on, princess, let's get you settled in. You'll love the room I'm going to put you in," Kira said linking her arm in mine and walking me through the hostel. I smiled to myself and felt the sun on my face. Maybe this isn't going to be as bad as I thought it would be, I thought to myself.

Chapter 2

I was given my room key and shown which bunk was mine before I unpacked a few things, had a shower and crashed in my bed. I had the bottom bunk and liked that I had a window behind my bed. I was also happy that I had been given a room where no other backpackers were in and thought that it was strange they would have so much space in the hostel that I could have my own room.

When I woke, it was night time and raining. Great, cold, just what I was trying to avoid, I thought as I pulled a jumper over my singlet and slid on my flip flops. Opening the door, I was happy to see Kira's familiar face.

"Hey princess, I was just coming to look for you, how are you feeling after your nap?" Kira said, handing me a wrist band and laughing when I didn't put it on.

"Here," she said, taking my wrist in her

hands and sticking the wrist band down.

"You really are just the sweetest. Come on, there's a movie night tonight, and it might be good for you to meet someone else. Do you like popcorn? It's backpacker style, homemade using 55cent popcorn kernels, but it tastes just as good," Kira said, taking my hand and walking me to the common room. I liked how soft her touch was, she made me smile, and I needed that right now. The heartbreak I was running away from feeling like a black dog at my back. My ex and I had broken up because she was just so depressive and bad for my general wellbeing and I hated having to leave her when I felt like she needed me. But I had learned that I wasn't in charge of how she felt, she was, and if she wasn't going to do the things that would help her, nothing I could do would help her either. Walking into the common room, I took a deep breath, smelling the buttery homemade popcorn and was handed a beer by an angry-looking girl with piercings up her ears.

"Here, I'm Danni," the girl said, opening the

beer for me.

"Hey, I'm Sasha," I replied, drinking happily, tasting a type of beer I had never had before. It felt nice to be here. Danni walked past me, giving Kira a knowing look, and I laughed, thinking that Kira must be the fuckgirl or something around here. I couldn't blame her she had the perfect hunting ground for it. I grabbed a bowl of popcorn and sat down next to some Germans who just smiled at me, and I nodded my head at them as they passed me a blanket as we all settled in and watched the movie. It was some stupid chick flick that I would never pay to watch, but it felt nice throwing popcorn at the TV when the two main characters kissed and laughing along with people I had never met before. I was aware that Kira had been watching me as she walked in and out of the common room. After the movie, I got into a game of hostel monopoly as I drank with Danni. I liked that Kira had continued to steal looks. I didn't really mind. In fact, it excited me.

"Are you teaching her all my tricks?" Kira

said, coming and sitting behind me. She had her legs on either side of me and wrapped her arms around my waist as she cuddled me and I was taken by surprise with how touchy-feely she was. She must have felt my body tense up because she turned me around slightly so I could look at her when she spoke.

"I'm super handsy. If you hate it, just say so, OK?" Kira explained. Making Danni smirk and roll her eyes.

"She does this with everyone, don't worry. If someone comes up to you and slaps your ass randomly, it'll be Kira," Danni said, making Kira gasp in playful shock.

"But you're just so cute. I hope you don't mind," Kira quickly added, making me relax and lean into her as she held me. I must admit, it felt nice to have someone showing me affection again, even if she did do it to everyone. Danni and I played the game well into the night, only getting up to get drinks and packets of chocolates from the vending machine. I bit my lip at one stage, excited when Kira patted her lap and pulled me down as I continued to play. It was just after midnight when the common room was closed, and Kira walked me back to my room.

"Goodnight, princess," Kira said wrapping her arms around me. I held her firmly, almost desperately not wanting to let her go.

"Oh, sweetie, are you OK?" Kira said taking my key from my hands and opening the door, taking my hand and pulling me into my room and shutting the door behind us. The room was dark, only the moonlight coming through my window shining on the white wall as Kira sat down on one of the empty beds with me.

"Tell me what's going on, princess," Kira said sitting opposite me but leaning forward to brush my hair out of my face. She looked serious, almost as though she was genuinely concerned, and I laughed at how stupid I felt getting sucked into her.

"I'm just exhausted, I'm OK," I tried to say to her as she shook her head.

"No, tell me the truth, princess, don't try and lie to me," Kira said making me curl my toes.

"You have to stop that," I whispered, biting my lip. I looked at Kira who just smiled knowingly.

"But aren't you a little princess Sasha?" She teased. I rolled my eyes and got up, surprised when Kira grabbed my wrist and pulled me back down. Holding my face in her hands, she kissed me, making me gasp as she stood up and pushed me against the wall as she kissed down my neck.

"Is this what you want, princess?" Kira said as she reached into my pants and gently rubbed my pussy over my panties. I pushed her away. I hadn't been touched like that in years.

"Get out," I quietly said, going to the door. Kira rolled her eyes and kissed my forehead on the way out.

"You know where to find me if you get scared, princess," Kira said as she left my room and made her way back to hers. I shut the door and climbed into my bed, shutting my eyes, and tried to get some sleep.

I tossed and turned all night. Every time I got close to falling asleep, a new sound would wake me up, or the memory of Kira would come back to my mind. Why did I refuse her? It felt great, I thought to myself, confused as to why I kicked her out. At 3 in the morning, I decided to go for a walk to the beach. Getting up I put on some warm pants, and a pullover found my glasses and tied my hair in a messy bun. I opened the door to my room and used my phone as a torch as I made my way down the clearing to the beach. I was not disappointed. The air was cool and salty, and the light breeze had a thin layer of sand lifting up as I took each step. The waves looked blue and black as they crashed, and for the first in what felt like forever, I felt totally at peace. Walking along the beach I was aware that someone was walking in the opposite direction. I walked down to the water's edge, hoping to avoid them.

"Sasha?" I heard her voice before I saw her. I was nervous. Why would she be out here this late?

"Kira?" I asked back.

"Princess, I thought you'd be all tucked up in bed, what are you doing?" Kira asked, hugging me. It was actually more me hugging her, and I liked that I took her by surprise as I held her tightly, like she was the answer to questions I didn't know I had. She smiled and kissed my forehead as she stroked my hand and let me hold her.

"I could ask you the same thing," I finally said, sitting down on the sand. I dug into the cold sand with my toes and shivered as the air whipped around us. Kira opened her oversize zip-up jacket, and I snuggled into her. I didn't care if she did this with everyone. I needed her to do this with me.

"I like going for walks at night. I feel the night calling to me sometimes, so I just go with it," Kira said. I was impressed with how open she was about who she was. She didn't seem to hide anything. Looking at me, I could tell Kira wanted an answer from me now.

"My reason is really lame, I just couldn't sleep," I said, shrugging my shoulders. Kira laughed and pulled me in closer.

"That's not lame princess," she said, pressing my head down until it was resting on her shoulder. As we looked out over the ocean, a liked that I could almost hear her heartbeat and feel her breath on me as silence came between us.

"How long have you been here?" I asked her, breaking the silence that had come between us.

"4 years. I came out as a backpacker but fell in love with it and stayed after I was sponsored," Kira explained.

"Was it easy?" I asked, interested in the process. Kira shook her head.

"Nothing good is ever easy, princess," she said laughing.

"It took three years of back and forth paperwork, but I'm here now, and I'm happy I can stay," Kira said in a serious voice I hadn't heard her use.

"Why, are you thinking of staying?" Kira asked, suddenly excited again. I looked at her before I kissed her deeply, surprised with myself, but happy when I heard her moan in my mouth.

"Maybe," I whispered as I pushed her back on the sand. I moved my body on top of her and kissed her until I had run out of ways to kiss her as dawn broke behind us over the ocean and lit up the beach. Kira rolled me over, obviously not wanting to be on her back anymore and lay down by my side as she kissed me while we watched the sun move up into the sky.

"This is going to be an amazing day princess. I can just tell," Kira said softly into my neck as she played with my hair.

Chapter 3

She wasn't joking. The day had been awesome. She had organized that everyone would go the jetty and jump off the end of it at lunchtime, followed by a big BBQ in the park. There was food and drinks and music, and I loved watching how she floated around the different groups of people. I had learned that she spoke five languages and she was always making someone laugh or telling them a story. I liked that she kissed me openly in front of people. I had learned that things moved very fast around here, and slight attraction turned into a full-blown relationship after a few hours of staring at each other.

"It's just the way when everyone is living together," Danni explained to me as I asked her how long another couple had been together, laughing when 3 hours came her response. I had hoped that Kira wouldn't use me for a few hours and then get rid of me when a new girl turned up — being relieved when Danni shook her head.

"You guys are as good as married now. She won't leave you. She never leaves; it's the other girls who go. When is your flight out?" Danni said, raising an eyebrow at me as the reality that I would be leaving too settled in.

"In two months time," I said quietly as Danni nodded her head as she drank.

"See?" She added as I got up and walked over to where Kira was playing in the playground.

"Hey, princess, having fun?" She asked making me feel like the only person in the world all over again. She laughed as she grabbed my hand and pulled me to the swings.

"Sit, let me swing you," Kira said, pulling my hips down onto the swing. I closed my eyes as she started to pull me back, forcing my mind not to go there. I knew what was just behind my eyes and as I opened them again I felt it hit. It was like a drug, her motherly nature, the way she called me princess, and the way she made me feel as she swung me high into the air, catching me every time I came back. I wondered if she knew what she was doing to me, what headspace she had me in constantly. I wondered if she would still like me if she knew.

The BBQ finished and walking back to the hostel. Kira grabbed my hand as I was about to walk out onto the road.

"Hold Mama's hand, princess," Kira laughed as a car sped past. The people around us didn't seem to care, but I almost died hearing those words. A guy grabbed a girl's hand and told her to hold Daddy's hand, and everyone laughed. Oh, it was just a joke. Everyone is joking. I said to myself trying to calm down. Kira looked at me with a gleam of mischief in her eye, and I looked at her quickly before looking down at the ground as she led me back to the hostel. Stopping outside my room, I could tell she wanted to come in, but I turned to look at her.

"I'm just really tired, probs still the jetlag, I think I'm just going to have a nap and maybe see you later?" I said as she held my hips and swayed me gently.

"Or maybe you're tired because you're a little princess and need Mama to let you have a nap?" Kira said, smiling, before kissing my cheek and walking away.

I took my clothes off and put them in the wash bag I had set up on the end of my bunk and walked into the shower, turning the water on and letting it pour over me. I was happy I had brought my own shampoo and conditioner and washed my hair for the first time since arriving. I lathed shower gel over my body, enjoying how it felt rubbing over my tits before I exfoliated and got out. I dried myself and hung my towel up before walking back into the room, surprised to see Kira sitting on my bed.

"Kira, what the fuck!" I screamed as I tried to cover up. I reached behind me to try and get my towel, and Kira jumped off my bed and grabbed my wrist, pulling my naked body to my bed.

"I can't let my little princess go to for naps

without a diaper, what kind of Mama would that make me?" Kira said, making me freeze.

"What did you just say?" I asked, making her laugh.

"I knew you were a baby the minute I saw you, princess, why do you think Mama spent all that special time with you?" Kira said, moving my body as she sprinkled the powder over me. My mind was lost for words, so I just lay there and let her diaper me, trying to fight the headspace she was forcing me back into.

"But," was all I could say as she pulled up my pajama pants over my fresh diaper and tickled me before putting on my long sleeve pajama shirt.

"Gosh, what a cute little princess for Mama," Kira said looking at me laying on my back, my thighs pushed apart by the thick diaper she had just put me in.

"Come on, time for pretty little princess naps," Kira said. She lay beside me, making me snuggle into her chest as her arms wrapped around me.

"No wonder you couldn't sleep last night little princess, Mama wasn't here then, but I'm here now," Kira said, stroking my hair as I fell asleep in her arms.

When I woke up, Kira was still cuddling me but was on her phone, scrolling through social media.

"Hi, princess," she said kissing my cheeks. I blinked sleepily at her, which just made her squeeze me tighter, and I tilted my head back to see what time of day it was. The first stars had just come out, but the sky was still light blue, so I knew it wasn't too late. Kira placed her hand on my diaper and frowned.

"Princess, you are still dry," she said, making me silently beg her not to make me wet my diaper. Kira reached into her bag and pulled out a baby bottle filled with water and rubbed the nipple over my lips, getting cross when I didn't open.

"Don't be a silly girl for Mama, drink up my little princess," Kira said, spanking my thigh until I opened my mouth as she held the bottle as I drunk.

"Good little princess for Mama," Kira said slowly, enjoying how I looked looking up at her. She placed her hand on my bladder and pushed down, making my eyes go wide as I drank.

"Don't try and fight Mama princess, you can wet your diaper here, or I'll take you out there and you can keep it on until you wet it in front of everybody, which do you want," Kira said, smiling when I began to slowly wet my diaper, getting embarrassed and looking away.

"Oh, does Mama's little princess not like wetting herself," Kira said taking the empty bottle out of my mouth. I shook my head and brought my arms up to my face, covering my eyes from her. Kira ran her hands up and down my body before gently taking my hands away.

"Alright, sweetie, Mama likes it, though. Come on, let's get you all cleaned up so you can go play all night," Kira said taking my hand and leading me into the bathroom. She took my pajama's off followed by my diaper, and I stood in the shower as she washed me.

"All clean now, little princess," Kira said passing me a new dry towel.

"What do you want me to wear Mama," I said, making Kira beam with delight.

"Oh, you are such a good little princess!" She exclaimed, going through my clothes and taking out a pair of baggy ripped jeans and a tight singlet.

"This will look so cute on you little princess, and when you get tired, there's enough room in here to put you in a diaper, and no one will even know," Kira said, playfully spanking my bottom as she dressed me.

Chapter 4

The days began to have a happy routine to them, and I started to find my place within the crazy hostel. Kira would organize events a week in advance, so there was always something to look forward too. So far we had gone on nature walks, seen wildlife, and gone snorkeling along the reef. Next week we were all going skydiving, and I had finally mastered the tricks in winning hostel monopoly. I had gotten used to Kira diapering me during my nap times in the middle of the day, and she had even started to make me wear one in the night. She had moved into my room and would cuddle me as I slept and choose what I would wear during the day.

"This one, Mama?" I asked her holding up a bikini. It was hot today, but we were still going to the beach to have a bonfire that night. Kira had to go early to help set it up, which meant that I was going early too. Kira said I could go for a swim while they set it all up and that if I was good, she wouldn't put a limit on the number of roasted marshmallows I could have.

"No, the other one princess," Kira said, coming out of the shower and towel drying her long blonde hair. I picked up the more revealing bikini but was stopped by Kira, who wanted to dress me instead.

"Such a slutty little princess for Mama, I'm going to enjoy watching you in this tonight," Kira said, tying my red bikini around my neck. It was a halter style and made my cleavage look like I had porn star tits the way it shaped me. The tiny, Brazilian cut bikini bottoms didn't leave much to be imagined and rubbed my clit when I sat down. When I had told Kira this, she had made me wear them to a picnic in the rainforest. She let me have my small pair of offcut high waisted denim shorts on as we walked through the rainforest, but made me take them off and sit on her lap during the picnic, enjoying my slight moans and begs for her to touch me. She had subtly spread my thighs under the table and reached down, lazily stroking me while she played cards with Danni, enjoying my squirms and soft grinds on her lap wanting more. I hoped she would do something like that tonight as well.

We arrived at the beach, and Kira kissed me before slapping my ass as I walked down the beach to the water. It was nice to cool down after such a hot day, and I dived under waves until I was tired and made my way back up to the beach. Laying down on my towel, I dried in the afternoon sun and fell asleep under the shade of a palm tree as the bonfire was starting to be lit.

"Come on, sleepyhead, either come and play or let Mama take you to bed," Kira said coming over and kissing me before whispering in my ear.

"I'll come over Mama," I said, waking up to her touch. She had sat next to me, blocking anyone's view of where her hand was and turned me over, so I was on my back looking up at her.

She grabbed at my body, looking down at me like she would take me right there. She slipped her fingers into my bikini bottoms and parted my pussy lips with her fingers before subtly toying with my cunt.

"Stay nice and quiet for Mama, little princess," Kira said as I placed my hands over my mouth. I was happy I had chosen a spot that was away from the bonfire and the partying going on around it, but I could still hear the laughter of my friends as they danced and drank. I moaned, and Kira slapped my tits to silence me.

"I said be quiet, princess," she hissed. I hadn't heard her be angry at me before, and I whimpered, not wanting to hear that voice again. She teased me, sliding in and out, just enough to make me wet but not enough to cum for what seemed like forever until she bent down and kissed me.

"Tell Mama how badly you need to cum princess," Kira said, finger fucking me slightly harder.

"Mama, please," I moaned in a breathless whisper. Kira laughed in satisfaction as she began to fuck me harder. Rubbing my clit with her thumb and sucking on my nipples, biting them gently as I bucked my hips against her hand. She was tall and skinny, and I was surprised that she could push me down with such strength. I was curvier than she was and had just assumed that I was stronger, but as she pinned me to the ground and made me take her until my orgasm was over, I knew that she was not someone to mess with.

"Pretty little princess," Kira said, putting her cum covered fingers in my mouth.

"Taste yourself, princess, lick Mama's fingers clean," Kira instructed, making me gag slightly before she took her fingers out of my mouth. I reached up, and Kira cuddled me, letting me nuzzle into her neck and watch the party from the safety of her lap as she cuddled me.

"Ready to go party little princess? Did Mama fuck you enough to make that slutty little pussy of yours not seek out attention from anyone else?" Kira said, cupping my cum soaked bikini bottoms, rubbing me predatorily. I just nodded into her neck and felt her kiss my cheek as she moved, motioning for me to get up and follow her to the fire.

We danced and drank and skinny-dipped in the water well into the night, with couple after couple leaving to fuck either back at the hostel or somewhere along the bush lined banks of the beach. I ate my fill of marshmallows, and Kira enjoyed showing me off, ripping my bikini top off and grabbing my tits in front of some boys who had only just moved into the hostel a day ago.

"You can look, but you can't touch my precious little princess. She's all Mama's," Kira said, making them laugh even though they didn't know what she was saying. I liked that Kira thought I was so special, and I really liked being shown off by her. We had talked about stuff like that, and Kira had said that she'd never do anything that made me overly embarrassed, but that she did like making me a little humiliated and had been excited when I told her that I found it hot to be on display. It felt nice to be with her, but I was aware that my flight back home was fast approaching. I had already been here a month, and I knew that I only had one month to go before I would have to say goodbye. The thought of leaving Kira torn at me. I had never had someone adore me as much as she did, and I just didn't know what to do about us.

Chapter 5

I had decided to go on a road trip before I had come to the hostel and had already arranged for a rental car to drive through the country to another big beach town.

"Everyone gets stuck out there, make sure you tell Kira where you are going so that when you get stuck, we can come and bring your broken-down ass home," Danni said over breakfast a day before I was meant to be leaving. Kira had said how excited she was for me, but I could feel in her touch that she didn't want me to go. Mostly because all she did was touch me. If she wasn't holding my hand, she was sitting me on her lap or fucking me in my bed, the shower, or the secluded areas at the beach. She had even taken me to a nudist beach and fucked me in a cave we found. I hated that I made her feel like she was losing me.

"Has Kira said anything to you about not

wanting me to go?" I asked Danni, making myself a coffee and eating some leftover pizza. Danni just shook her head.

"Nothing, the only thing she said, was that if she really loved you like she claims, that she'd have to let you go because she would never deserve you if she couldn't give you what you needed or wanted," Danni replied.

"That's not nothing!" I said in shock. I had no idea how deep her affection for me was. Danni shrugged her shoulders as she got up.

"Try not to worry about it too much, she always knew you'd leave Sasha," she said before going back into the kitchen and washing her dishes. Kira had gone to the airport to pick up the new people who were arriving today, and I knew she'd be gone for another hour as I took my coffee cup and headed for the beach.

I walked up and down the beach, drinking my coffee, wondering how on earth I was meant to go on without her. It's the biggest mistake leaving her, I thought, thinking about how she had given me something that most people couldn't. How rare it was to find someone as attractive as Kira, who wanted me, who also was a Mommy Domme. They don't just appear Sasha. You know that! I yelled at myself, looking out over the ocean. The waves were rough today, almost as rough as my heart was feeling. I sat down and watched as they crashed onto the shore, bringing in rocks and big shells from the depths of the ocean and smashing them down.

"I thought I might find you here," a familiar voice said, coming behind me. Kira sat down, her legs on either side of me, and pulled me into her, wrapping her arms around me and kissing me gently behind my ear.

"I need to say this selfishly. Don't go, little princess," Kira said, her voice shaky. I dipped my head and hated how this felt. I turned in her arms and put my head to her chest.

"Come with me," I whispered as she held me to her, her hand on the back of my head, making me breathe in her scent of coconut tanning oil and ocean spray. She looked down at me and brought my mouth to hers, kissing me deeply.

"I can't. I have to stay here, princess," she said breaking the kiss.

"But why?" I asked. I knew I sounded whiney, and I knew she hated that, but I didn't care, I didn't want to leave without her. I didn't want to live without her.

"Because I have to work. It might look like I'm having one big holiday, but I get paid by the hour princess, Mama is working, even now. I can't just take a month off and go with you. I could take like a week, max, but that would only be if it was approved, and they would have to find someone to replace me, and it's way too short notice," Kira said, explaining everything to me. I nodded.

"Then I just won't go," I said confidently. Kira laughed and shook her head.

"You have to go, princess. You only have a short time left here, and I don't want you to be here just because I don't want to lose you," Kira said running her hands over my tits.

"You could never lose me, Mama," I said, feeling my heartbreak. I knew then that I had to go, I knew that this would be the last time I kissed her lips as I felt her tongue in my mouth gently teasing me as tears streamed down both our cheeks.

On the day I left, Kira woke early and took my diaper off me in silence, kissed my forehead, and left the room. I waited for her to come back, but she never did. Packing my things into the back of a taxi, I tried not to cry as I helped the taxi driver put my things in the boot and hugged my friends goodbye. I looked for Kira, but she wasn't there, and I ground my teeth trying to stay strong as the taxi driver drove me to the car rental place. Danni had said that she'd say goodbye from me to Kira when she saw her, but I knew that we had already said goodbye.

I got to the car rental place, picked up my car, and began driving through the city and onto the high way. I realized that I had never gotten the photo of my ex back from Kira, and I laughed, thinking of how stupid I was forever wasting my time on a girl who thought drinking her problems away would solve anything. I drove along the highway, listening to music and thinking about Kira. How she had always made sure I had enough snacks and drinks, I looked around to see that I hadn't packed anything to eat or drink and wished she was here to look after me as I pulled into a gas station and bought some snacks. Walking back out to the car, I felt my phone vibrate in my pocket. I looked at the caller, happy it was Kira.

"Hey! I was just thinking about you," I said excitedly.

"I bet you were turn around," Kira said. I smiled, my tummy instantly full of butterflies as I slowly turned. Getting kissed full on the lips, I felt Kira's arms wrap around me, holding me tightly and squishing the snacks into me, making my bag of chips pop and fall out onto the floor.

"I guess Mama owes you some chips now, hey princess," Kira said taking the things out of my hands.

"But how?!" I said excitedly.

"I pulled some strings. I meant it when I said I couldn't let you go," Kira said, taking the car keys from my hand and jingling them in front of me.

"Mind if I drive?" She said as I just nodded silently.

"How did you get here?" I asked as we dropped the snacks into the car. I noticed that she didn't have anything with her. She looked back and pointed to Danni, who just waved and took Kira's bag out of her car.

"Surprise!" Danni said, making me run over to her and punch her shoulder.

"I was in tears, you bitch!" I said, making her laugh.

"Yeah, I know, I felt really bad actually, but I knew that you'd like this, so, yay," Danni said. We said goodbye, this it was a far happier departure, and Kira buckled me in before we drove out of the gas station.

"Were you just going to keep going until I stopped?" I asked her, pouring the drink I had bought into the bottle Kira had instructed me too.

"Yeah, that was pretty much my plan. I knew you'd be stopping pretty soon. I knew you wouldn't have packed any snacks," she said, sighing contentedly as she pushed my bottle into my mouth.

"It feels good to be here alone with you princess, Mama is going to love this," Kira said, pulling my seat down and making me have a nap as she drove.

Chapter 6

We stopped into a motel as the day ended. Kira had driven 6hours, only stopping to change me into a diaper at the side of the road, which she enjoyed immensely.

"I'd love it if someone stopped behind us and saw what I was doing to you, princess," Kira said, taking longer to redress me, enjoying how I looked on the back seat, diapered and sucking my thumb.

She took my hand and rubbed my ass as we walked into the motel reception, got our keys, and made our way to the room.

"This looks really nice, good call princess," Kira said, opening the door and looking around. I was happy she liked my choice. We had passed a number of motels along the way, and I had said all of them looked gross. This one had a pool, which was the only reason I had picked it, so I was glad when Kira also approved.

"Let's get you all clean and ready for bed, princess. You'll have to wet that diaper for Mama first though," Kira said taking out our shower things and laying out the onesie she had bought for me along with a fresh love heart diaper. I shook my head, not wanting to wet my diaper, and Kira laughed in shock that I would refuse her.

"Oh, is that how you want to play it, little princess?" She said grabbing my neck and bending me over her lap. She didn't give me any warning as she spanked my ass, making me squeal and squirm on her lap.

"Be a quiet little princess, or I'll open the door and let everyone see why you are making so much noise," Kira said, making me half believe that she wasn't making empty threats. She kept spanking me until she felt me wet my diaper. My head bowed in defeat, and she patted me gently until I finished.

"Good girl. You can stay like that though until Mama has finished her shower, and maybe if you good for me next time, I'll change you straight away, princess," Kira said, making me sit down on the floor and watch as she showered. I loved watching her slender body turn in the water, and her hands glide over her body as she washed. I wouldn't think that she could be a Mama upon looking at her. She had the typical, straight white girl look going on, with on-trend clothes and a beach babe style, she was certainly not the kind of woman I would have thought would want to be Mommy, let alone my Mama. But she was, and I loved how cool she was. Whenever we went anywhere, boys would always hit on her, but she would just playfully turn them down and cuddle up to me instead. I had asked her what she saw in me that she liked so much and was happy when she could give me a list.

"You are soft and cute, with your little tummy and these big titties and this thick jiggly butt that Mama loves to play with. You are quiet, and when you're slutty, you're slutty just for Mama, which I love too. I like that you are clever and that you read books instead of wanting to watch movies and I think your glasses are just so cute. I like that you're a little princess and don't like to get messy or dirty. Sasha, you're so lovable, all I want to do is smother you in Mama's love, wrap you in my arms and never let you go. You make me feel like a Mama. You get me in that headspace the minute I look at you, and I love it!" She had said, making me blush and tear up with happiness, which just made her kiss me all over and shake my tits in her hands.

Kira finished in the shower and looked at me, frowning back at her.

"Oh, is someone pouty with Mama princess?" Kira asked pulling on her pajama shorts and shirt. I nodded and crossed my arms looking angrily at the floor.

"Well, be a good girl next time and do what Mama says the first time I say it silly girl, and this won't happen to you. Come on, crawl to the bathroom for me," Kira instructed watching me crawl to her. She reached down and rolled me over, taking off my jeans and diaper making me happy it was off.

"Get in," she kindly said, turning the water on for me. I loved that she always managed to find the right temperature, and I washed myself in front of her as she played with her pussy.

"You are making Mama horny little princess," Kira said as she stopped herself just as she was about to cum.

"You can finish me off with that pretty tongue of yours when you get out," she said, turning my shower off and rubbing me down with my towel. She took me to the queen-sized bed and laid me down, before putting my love heart diaper on and clipping my short sleeve onesie up. I loved how it felt and ran my hands over my tits, making her laugh.

"Little princess, take those hands away and put them behind your head for Mama," Kira said, climbing on top of me. I hadn't realized she had taken her pants off until her wet pussy was on my lips as she began to make me kiss and suck her, grinding on my face.

"You'll be a good girl and make Mama cum little princess," Kira moaned as she rode my face. I licked her slit and sucked on her clit, flicking my tongue against it, worshiping her pussy. I reached my tongue into her pussy as far as it would go and liked that I could feel her shudder as her cum covered my tongue. I kept licking and sucking her, making her grind down harder, making me gasp for air.

"I'm sorry little princess," Kira said, lifting off me slightly and reaching back to play with my tits. She shook them, holding them by my nipples as she came again, this time grabbing my tits as she did, making me moan into her pussy. She must have liked the vibration of my moan because she grabbed at my tits, again and again, making me moan into her and against her clit.

"Fuck little princess, you're so good for Mama," Kira moaned, lifting off my mouth and coming to lie down next to me. She kissed my lips and licked them, tasting herself. She smiled at me, wrapping her arms around me and pulling me in close to her.

"Look how cute you are, princess," Kira said rubbing the front of my onesie and kissing me all over my face.

"Stay there," Kira instructed as she went into the bathroom and wet a corner of the towel, coming back other to me and wiping my face clean.

"I can't have my little princess being all dirty, can I baby?" Kira said, delighting me that I didn't have to stay dirty. She pulled the bedsheets down and tucked me in before turning the lights off and coming back into bed, letting me snuggle into her. I felt her ribs against my tits, and she ran her fingers through my soft hair.

"Sweet dreams, princess," Kira said as she began to stroke the side of my breast.

"I'm happy I have you back, Mama," I replied getting gently squeezed as I fell asleep to her gently groping hands.

Chapter 7

We had left in the morning at nine and had driven for four hours before we noticed that the fuel light was dangerously low.

"Look up where a station is on Mama's phone, baby," Kira said passing me her phone. She had put me in a fresh diaper and told me just to get used to being in them, stating that she would only let me use the bathroom for emergencies. I was happy she knew my limits and didn't try to push them. She had dressed me a summer dress and sandals, but let me take them off when we were driving, and I could cross my legs on the seat.

"There's one about an hour away, Mama," I said showing her the phone just before we lost reception.

"Ok, well, we will just have to make it," Kira said, putting her foot down. There was nothing but red dirt on either side of us on this long stretch of road, and I wondered what would happen if we broke down. Kira drove ten over the speed limit, and I hoped that she would get us there in time.

"What happens if we don't make it, Mama?" I asked, holding Kira's hand and turning down the stereo. Kira gave me a funny look.

"We will have to walk little girl, and don't think for a second that'll mean I let you put on your big girl panties," she said, looking back at the road. Her phone beeped, reception returning but just as the car began to slow down. Kira looked at me, rolled her eyes and sighed. I was happy it wasn't an angry sigh, and I looked at her with wide eyes.

"I hope you like walking little princess," Kira said as she pulled over to the side of the road and parked. I looked at her and then looked out into the emptiness of the land.

"But Mama," I said as she unbuckled my seat belt and pushed a paci in my mouth.

"Complain, and I'll make you suck it all the way, so everyone will know you're a naughty little girl for her Mama, is that what you want?" Kira said. I shook my head, and Kira groped at my tits for a while before taking the paci out of my mouth and putting it in her bag. We got out of the car and felt the hot sun on our skin immediately before we put our water and snacks in our bags and started to walk to the gas station we knew was only a few kilometers ahead.

"What if they are closed, Mama?" I asked, holding her hand.

"Well then, we figure out a plan B princess," Kira said.

"I'm happy you're here, Mama," I said kissing her.
We walked for an hour before we stopped to put on more sun cream and had a drink.

"It shouldn't be much further, baby girl," Kira said, reaching her hand out to me and waiting for me catch up to her.

"We can get a nice cold ice-cream when we get there, we have definitely deserved it!" She added, wiping the sweat off her forehead. We continued walking for another hour before we saw a truck coming behind us. Usually, I wouldn't have wanted it to stop with nowhere to run, but it was hot, so I just hoped that we wouldn't be in any danger. The truck slowed and stopped in front of us, and I squeezed Kira's hand firmly scared of what would happen next.

"It's OK princess, Mama is here, you'll be fine," Kira said. I was relieved to see that it was a woman who got out of the truck, but surprised when I saw what type of woman it was. She was hot! The type of hot that you'd find as a pin-up model in a tattoo artist back room. She wore ripped denim shorts and a baggy muscle singlet. Walking confidently to us, she smiled and stuck out her hand at Kira.

"Looking little lost girls?" She said, shaking Kira's hand and then mine.

"I'm Mel, saw what I'm guessing is your car a little while back. Where you headed?" Mel said. I liked that Kira took over, I was pretty sure I had heat stroke and found it hard even to stand up.

"We were going to Paradise Island, but our car's out of gas. We thought there was a station up here," Kira said. I held Kira's hand, and Mel smiled at me.

"Well, I don't think she'll last much longer in this heat. Let me drive you to the station and then back to your car. It'll be a long walk yet. They've just moved another half hour's drive north, which will mean you'd be walking an awful long way and back," Mel explained. Kira gladly accepted, and Mel helped me into the cab of her truck, letting me lie down and have a rest in the cold aircon as she drove us.

"Thanks for this," I heard Kira said. I closed my eyes and was happy that I hadn't done this trip alone, Danni was right, everyone breaks down along this trip.

"It's alright. Your friend is cute," Mel said to Kira, who just turned around to look at me.

"Yeah, she's lovely," Kira said. That was the last thing I heard before I fell asleep. When I woke up, it was dark, and I had rolled onto my tummy, my dress had ridden over my ass, my puffy diaper on full display. I tried to open my eyes, but everything was black. I tried to move, but my arms and legs were tied, making me splay across Mel's bed. I tried to yell, but there was a gag in my mouth. *I knew we shouldn't have gotten a lift from her!* I thought hoping that she wasn't hurting Kira. I began to cry. Hot tears rolled down my cheeks and onto the bed as I felt hands moved the back of my legs. I tried to scream, but only muffled sounds came out, crying harder.

"Shh, it's OK, princess Mama has you, you're alright, baby," I heard Kira say. I relaxed and whimpered, wanting to see her and cuddle her.

"Mama just tied you up because you looked so cute laying there. You will never believe it, Mel is a Mommy too!" Kira said, sounding very excited. She had told me she had tried to find friends in the scene but hadn't had any luck. Clearly, she had been successful here. I heard a door open, and Mel climb inside, closing it behind her.

"Oh, has she woken up?" Mel asked Kira

who just patted my ass.

"Yes, she has," Kira replied with a voice I knew meant that I was about to be fucked. I felt Kira loosen the ties around my legs and arm before she turned me around so that I was on my back.

"Do you want to play little princess?" Kira asked. I thought for a minute before nodding yes. I liked that Kira asked. I liked that I knew I could say no. She made me feel so protected and loved. She knew getting bound in my sleep was one of my fantasies, and I loved that she had been so bold to try and make it come true.

"Can Mel touch you, princess? Kira asked, kissing my neck, slowly pulling off the blindfold. I let my eyes adjust until they could see Mel. She smiled down at me, and I blushed as I nodded yes making her smile.

"Thank you, baby girl," Mel said, slowly stroking my thigh. I liked that she let me get used to her touch before she tried anything else, and I moaned and wriggled against the gag and the ties.

"No, I think you're going to need to stay like that baby girl. You're going to make too much noise if we take this out," Kira said, grabbing the strap of the gag and making my head shake. She grabbed the bottom of my dress and wriggled it up to my body until it was over my tits making Mel raise an eyebrow and smile hungrily at me.

"May I?" Mel said, asking Kira, who just smiled.

"She likes it like this," Kira said, pulling the front of my bra down and pulling out my tits by my nipples, making me squeal.

"Cute baby," Mel said, slapping my tits and flicking my nipples. She was stronger than Kira, and I felt her touch on my clit as she licked my nipples until I tried to pull away from her. Kira rubbed my pussy over my diaper as Mel held my neck down and continued to lick my nipples, going from left to right, only stopping to bend down and suck them firmly, biting them as she pulled them up before going back to flicking them. I arched my back and moaned loudly, feeling the start of an orgasm building. Kira took off my diaper and tossed it the side before spitting on my pussy and sliding her strap-on against me, pulling it back and letting it hit against my clit.

"I think she likes that," Kira said to Mel, who had started slapping my tits and groping them. Kira spat on my pussy again before sliding her cock into me as Mel rubbed my clit, making me cum instantly.

"You have to still ask for permission, little princess. I don't care if you're gagged, you won't have such bad manners," Kira said as she began pounding into me. I knew she was mad I hadn't asked by the force she was putting behind her thrusts. I started begging her to let me cum, squealing when I felt Mel lift me up and slide our thin dildo into my ass.

"I wouldn't let her if she was my baby girl," Mel said as she matched Kira's thrusts. Mel turned me in her lap so that she and Kira were fucking me from the side. I felt Kira grab my ass and shake it in her hand.

"Oh, she won't be cumming, and if she does, Mama is going to tied her hand behind her back and let strangers finger fuck her until she is crying for them to stop. Isn't that right baby girl," Kira said as I bit down hard on the gag and held off my orgasm.

We had come up with punishments, but she had only ever spanked me and made me stand in the corner, this was a punishment we had come up with for when I was really naughty, so I guessed she was really mad that I had cum without permission. I nodded and moaned, holding off another orgasm. Tightening my abs for so long to hold off cumming began to make my tummy hurt as Kira and Mel used me. I had a sneaky feeling Kira was trying to make me cum as she grabbed my hair and pulled my head back, making me look at her.

"Be Mama's good little princess. Show Mama how good you can be," she said. Usually, these words would have sent me over the edge, but I refused to cum, letting Mel fuck my ass and rub my clit as Kira fucked my pussy. I smiled at Kira behind my gag and felt her lovingly stroke my face, I knew she knew I was only holding on by a thread and she leaned down, kissing my cheek but fucking me deeper.

"You can cum princess," Kira said, making me explode and squirt all over her as I relaxed my pussy and abs. Mel untied my hand and held my hand to her breast, making me squeeze and toy with her as her other hand refused to stop fucking me. I shuddered as my orgasm lasted longer than it ever had in my life and lay limp, my only movement, the forced groping of my hand on Mel's big breasts.

"What a pretty little-used slut," Kira said pulling out of me, only making my pussy juices drip out of my cunt as the aftershock of my orgasm ravaged through my body. Mel untied me and took the toy out of my ass and pulled my dress and bra off.

"What a good girl," Mel said, putting me in her lap and forcing her nipple in my mouth. She took me by surprise, and I pulled away, not knowing if Kira would be mad or not but settled when I felt her stroke my forehead.

"It's OK, princess, you can suck on Mel's juicy titties," Kira said lovingly. Mel was larger than Kira, and I felt small in her arms as she pushed more of her breast in my mouth. I was obedient to Kira because I loved her, but I was good for Mel because I knew I couldn't overpower her. I stayed sucking on her nipples until I began to close my eyes, weary after the fucking I had just been given and Kira came into Mel's arms and watched as I suckled.

"We'd make a cute little family," Mel laughed, wrapping her arm around Kira. Kira smiled and rubbed my tummy.

"Unfortunately, our little princess would be leaving us too soon though, she's going back home in a few weeks," Kira replied. I tried to speak, but Mel held my mouth to her nipple and gently slapped my face.

"I didn't say you were finished baby girl,"

she said, quieting me back down.

Chapter 8

Mel drove us to the gas station, and we filled two cans of petrol before she drove us back to our car. It was dark by the time we got there, and I could feel my pussy still leaking cum into the new diaper Mel had put me in.

"Thanks so much, Mel, we would have been really fucked if it hadn't of been for you," Kira said, hugging her goodbye. Mel reached out and stroked my hair as she held Kira.

"Well, somebody was fucked anyway," she said, making Kira laugh. I hugged Mel goodbye, letting her lift up the front of my dress and rub over my diaper one more time before we parted ways.

"Be a good girl for your Mama baby girl," Mel said, smiling at me. I nodded and sucked my thumb, reaching out to hold Kira's hand.

"Take care," Kira said, putting me into the

car.

"I liked her, Mama," I said as Kira drove us back onto the road. She looked at me and winked.

"That's good. I'm glad you had a good time. I had hoped that you'd like it, princess," Kira said rubbing my head.

The rest of the trip went like clockwork. We saw all the big tourist sites, figured out where the gas stations where before we ran out of fuel, and I took more photos than my camera and phone could hold. Kira and I ate at amazing restaurants, and I loved spending all my time with her. As we drove back to Waker's Beach, I knew that our time was ending, and it tore at me as it had done all those weeks ago.

"It's just so unfair, Mama," I said as Kira drove through the city. I knew we were only an hour away from the hostel and in three days I would be on a plane going back home. Kira looked at me with sad eyes.

"You could always come back next year?"

She said. I guess I could, but would it be the same? Would we be the same, or would we have found new people? I wasn't sure and decided to just look out the window until we got back to the hostel. The next two days were a blur as I saw the familiar faces, wondering if these people would ever leave. It the last day when Kira and I finally talked about what would happen after I left.

"So what do you want to do? Like realistically, where do you think this can go?" Kira said. I had taken her out to have coffee and cake at a café. This had become one of our favorite spots. The café was situated on the beachfront and we sipped our coffees looking out over the ocean. Surfers were catching the last waves of the day, and some of the backpackers were having a competition who could dig the biggest hole in the sand.

"I'll really miss this. I'll really miss you. We can stay in touch though, right?" I said looking at Kira. She had worn my favorite flowy beach dress, and her hair was done up in a half-bun. The sun had streaked her hair white blonde in some parts, and she looked down and smiled into her coffee.

"Of course we can princess," she said. I didn't know how to make it better. The ache I felt in my heart was unlike anything I had experienced before. I had weighed up all my options. To stay and try to get sponsored like she had done, to go and come back every year for holidays to see her. To have her fly over to see me in my home town. The wind picked up, and I shivered. None of those options were long-lasting and I could feel her slipping away from me.

"I have been thinking about things, though," Kira said making my stomach turn. We had played, everything will be the same game for so long, I was really hoping she wasn't about to shatter the façade.

"Maybe I could come and see you in a few months and see if we mesh just like we have here. Maybe some time apart once you have settled back into your daily routine, will make you realize that this was just a holiday thing, that you aren't really into it, and I could come over and see if I still fit in your world?" Kira said. It was the first time I had seen her nervous. She had always been in such control of every situation she had been in that seeing her so worried about my response made me realize she was just as nervous how parting ways as I was.

"I don't think this is a holiday thing, Mama," I said, leaning forward to call her Mama and making her smile. She reached for my hand and squeezed it tightly.

"But I'd love that. Maybe you even like my city and can find a job you like or something," I said, stopping myself as I began to race through the possibility of her moving to be with me. She just smiled and looked out at the glimmering ocean. The sun was setting behind us, and I knew that I had seen my last sunset as I looked through the café and out over the mountain range that was to our backs. Turning back around I saw that Kira had placed a letter on the table.

"Will you read it when you are back home?"

She asked, but I could only nod my head. I felt as if I would burst into tears if I spoke again, so I just looked down and looked at my letter. She had kissed it with red lipstick, and I held it as though it was the most special thing I had ever held. A waitress came to ask us if we wanted our cakes to go as they were closing, and I realized that we hadn't even touched them.

"That would be great thanks," Kira said and gave a fake smile to the waitress who walked away to get us containers.

Walking down the beach and back to the hostel, Kira linked her arm in mine as we talked about the last two months.

"I can't believe it's already over," she said, kicking the sand.

"I feel like it was only yesterday that I picked you up. I thought you were so cute how you kept falling asleep," Kira said, making me laugh.

"You have no idea how nervous you made me when you kept calling me princess and talking about yourself in the third person," I replied.

"Yeah, well, I knew you needed Mama to look after you, what can I say," Kira said, grabbing my tits and bending down to kiss them.

"I still can't believe you let me fuck you as you did. You're such a slutty princess for Mama. It made me really proud watching you let Mel fuck you," Kira added making me blush.

"Yeah, I'm surprised I did too. I guess you just make me feel really safe like even when I am nervous about something, I look at you and know it'll be alright," I said.

"Like wearing your diaper in public," Kira whispered as we walked through the hostel and back to our room. I giggled and turned around as she slapped my ass, and playfully grabbed my hips, pushing into my ass as I opened the door to our room.

Chapter 9

Even though I knew that Kira couldn't surprise me by being on my flight home like she had surprised me by coming on my road trip, I still had a glimmer of false hope as she drove me to the airport.

"I'm sorry, I can't stay. I tried, but they only let me have the shuttle as a favor, and it has to be back as soon as possible," Kira said as we drove. Usually, the shuttle was only for picking people up, but she had called in a favor so she could drive me.

"I know," I said. I held her hand as we drove, talking about when she would be able to video call and what I would do when I got home.

"I don't expect you to keep the rules I had for you here when you get back princess, I know you have a whole life there," Kira said, turning the radio down. I turned to look at her.

"But I want to Mama," I said more little than

I had liked. I was about to go on a flight by myself where I had to make sure I was safe, and at the right terminal, I didn't have time to be little. But holding onto Kira's hand made me feel like her princess, and that was all I wanted in the world. Kira looked at me and smiled.

"Keep my rules then, but let me know if you start to get rid of them, OK?" She asked. I could tell this was as hard for her as it was for me. A friend told me not to fall for anyone while I was away, and I had scoffed in their face saying as if I was that stupid, that I was only going for two months, and what on earth could happen in two months? Well, I was wrong, very wrong as I ached to stay with Kira for one more minute. We reached the airport, and I got out, forcing back my tears. I looked at her and tried to burn her image into my memory, her long blonde hair, tall slender body, mischievous brown eyes, and tanned skin. The way she smiled like she had a big secret she was just about to share and how her long arms wrapped around me as she held me tight. We stayed holding each other as silent tears rolled down our cheeks, being told twice by the security guards that she had to move on before she broke our embrace.

"Have a safe flight, princess," Kira said holding my face in her hands and stroking my tears away with her thumbs.

"I'll talk to you really soon, Mama," I said not caring who was around to hear. Kira smiled warmly, kissed me one more time before letting my face go and stepping back. She just nodded as she took a deep breath and walked back to the driver's side, honking the horn as she drove away. I stood there, watching her go, new tears forming in my eyes, Kira taking my heart away with her.

I made my way through customs, numbly followed the signs to my terminal, and sat, waiting to be let on the plane. *This sucks,* I thought, pouting and wanting her back. I was not looking forward to going home. I thought about my job, the things I did for entertainment, and it just didn't compare to the experiences I had had with Kira or even the beachside life in general. I thought about what I could do for work here and did a few internet searches on the types of visas that I was eligible for. I could study something and come on a student visa. *I'll just study the degree which has the longest duration.* I thought hopefully as I looked into how to apply for that. I heard my flight being called and walked over to the gates and took a deep breath as I made my way down the ramp and to my seat.

The flight was as annoying as the one coming over, and I took a sleeping pill so I could just sleep through the whole thing, waking up just in time to leave the plane. It felt so weird coming back. I had changed so much, but looking around, it felt like I was the only thing to have changed. I hailed a taxi, was driven back to my apartment, walked inside and sat on my couch.

"Well, I wasn't expecting that," I said out loud and looked around my place. I stood up and walked to the window and looked out onto the city street. I heard basketballs bouncing, cars honking their horns and people yelling, ambulance sirens rang down the street, and I turned away from the window, sad that I wasn't back in my laid back seaside home. I went to my suitcase and started unpacking as I found the letter Kira had given me. I ran my fingertips over her red lipstick kiss, remembering how her kiss had tasted and smiled, excited to be hearing from her.

Hi princess,

I guess you'll be home now and wondering what I'm doing. If you're not wondering what I'm doing, why not?! Mama should always be on your mind, cheeky girl! Anyway, I'm looking through our photos. I'll probably print some of them off and stick them around my room. I have claimed our old room as my room, I have to pay a little extra to have the whole room to myself, but I don't care, I couldn't cope if someone else was to sleep in here if it wasn't you. The days are starting to get cooler here, so you should be happy you got your pretty little tan while you did! It'll be sweater weather here before long

I put the letter down and grabbed the puppy Kira had bought me and pressed it into my face as tears began to fill my eyes. She had sprayed her perfume all over it, and my heart skipped a beat as I smelt her so close to me. I had decided that I would buy that perfume the minute I could and spray it over my pillows, so when I slept it would be like she was still with me. I took out my phone and messaged her straight away. Having a shower, I put on a fresh diaper and sent her a message of that too and was so happy when she replied. We messaged back and forth all night, and I fell asleep listening to a voice message she sent me, happy to have Mama back, even if it was through a screen.

Chapter 10

I went back to work the following Monday and answered everyone's questions about how my trip was and how they thought the photos I put up of skydiving and the nature that I had seen were so cool. I sat at my desk, looked at the pile of paperwork that had collected there. I opened the letters, was given a new project of photographing a sporting event and had several calls from past clients asking me to photograph this event and that event. By lunchtime, I had to walk out onto the street for some fresh air and wondered how I could have ever been happy living this life. I took my phone out and looked at Kira's social media accounts. She had gone fishing today and had caught a colorful fish, posing with it before writing a big spiel about how it's important to make sure the hook is out of the mouth of the fish before putting it back in the ocean. I smile as I scrolled through, looking at the photos of her organizing a beach clean up after a festival and how they had had a costume movie night. She had dressed up as a belly dancer, and I was pretty sure it was only so she could wear next to nothing. I saw Danni doing her usual angry glare in some photos and missed them terribly as I looked up and around my world. It was gray. Literally, the buildings were gray, the sky was gray, and the people were gray. No one looked happy to be here. No one smiled; no one's eyes shone with excitement. They just looked blankly faced, staring right through me as I looked in front and behind me. I looked at my phone again and knew I had to get back to her. I had to get back to Kira.

I knew I couldn't just get on a plane and head back. I knew that because I had no visa just to go back on, and I really didn't want to go back just to have to leave again so soon. I into the student visa again and applied. I choose an arts degree, majoring in photography, I figured I might as well do something I actually loved and who knows, maybe I would learn something new. The degree was four years, and I knew that I would have to return to this gray mess after I graduated, but I also figured that Kira and I would have a solid understanding of where we wanted to take our relationship by then. I paid for the visa and was happy I fulfilled all the medical and financial requirements. Now all I had to do was wait to hear if I got it or not.

Kira and I talked daily and fell into a routine really quickly with me messaging in my morning, and her messaging in her morning. That meant that I would message her when I woke up, and by the evening my time, I would get a response. I liked that nothing seemed to change with us. I had been worried that the distance would slowly start to break our relationship down. I had finally heard back about my visa status and was over the moon that I had been granted it and was set to start the degree in a months time. I booked my flight back to her, happy this time I was only booking a one-way ticket. I had decided not to tell her. I thought it would be better to surprise her by just showing up. I handed in my two weeks' notice to leave my job and was happy to be finally rid of this gray city. It had been three months since I had last held Kira and as I boarded my plane back to her, I could hardly keep a straight face.

It felt like coming home as I left the airport, the warm air hitting my face instantly. I had decided to take a taxi to the hostel. I didn't want Kira to see me until I casually strolled into the common room or something and clapped my hands excitedly as we pulled into Waker's Beach hostel. I had booked a room under a different name so that she wouldn't know it was me and grabbed my bags out of the boot of the taxi, inhaling deeply as my lungs filled with the sea breeze. I had sold all of my furniture before coming back, knowing that I wouldn't need it and looked at all my worldly possessions, which had been carefully packed into my three suitcases.

"No fucking way!" I heard, turning around to see Danni. She hugged me before I even had a chance to lift my arms and laughed, feeling more at home here than I had when I went back to my real home.

"Oh my god, Sasha! What are you doing here?!" She said squealing.

"I actually am studying here now. I'll be here for the next four years!" I replied happily, frowning when I realized that Danni was, in fact, still here.

"Um, what about you? Why or how are you still here?!" I asked. She just rolled her eyes.

"I got a shit house job, but they are sponsoring me, so meh, I just wanted to stay really," Danni replied making me laugh. She looked down at my bags before looking up at me.

"Does Kira know you've come back?" She asked cautiously, making me nervous.

"No, I thought that I'd make it a surprise," I said. Danni bit her lip, and I felt my stomach lurch instantly. *Was she with someone else? Had she moved? Had something awful happened to her?* I thought as I watched Danni.

"I think she'll be really happy to see you. But she's not the same girl you left behind," Danni said hesitantly. I just looked at her, waiting for an explanation but when one wasn't given, I looked at the ground nervously.

"Should I have not come back? Danni, will you just tell me if she's with someone else?!" I said angrily, feeling my voice become shaky.

"What?! No, nothing like that. She's completely obsessed with you! She's been in an accident though. She's at the hospital," Danni said relieving my fears.

"Take me there," I said, hoping Danni still had her car. She agreed, and I put my bags in my old room, happy to see Kira still had my photos on the wall and drove with Danni to the hospital.

"What kind of accident?" I asked nervously. I really hadn't wanted to ask, but I figured I needed to know what I was walking into. Kira hadn't posted anything online in a few days, but I hadn't thought that was strange. She had gone days without posting before.

"We went to the jetty to jump off the edge like we've done hundreds of times before. But this time, when she jumped, she jumped right in the way of a shark. It bit her and um," Danni said stopping and looking at me, making me hold my breath. Her face was white. She had clearly seen the whole thing.

"There was a lot of blood Sasha. And her screams, I'll never stop hearing them. By the time we got her to hospital," Danni said. I could tell she was reliving it.

"Do not fucking tell me she is dead. Do not!" I said as tears began to stream down my face. Danni just shook her head.

"She lost her arm, she lost so much blood she is in a coma, they don't know if she'll wake up," Danni said as we arrived at the hospital. I jumped out of the car and ran inside, asking where her room was, but I didn't have to. There were flowers and balloons around the fourth room I went past and looked through the window, my whole world stopping.

I don't know how long I stayed standing there for, but when I felt Danni's hand on my shoulder, I snapped out my daze.

"What?" I said, looking at Danni angrily.

"You can go in," Danni said. I was happy that she understood that I wasn't angry at her. I walked in slowly, Kira had a tube going down her throat, and the monitor was beeping every couple of seconds. I looked at her body and tried to take it all in. I couldn't seem to register that she had lost her arm, but there she was, lying in the bed, hooked up to a monitor, missing her arm. The shark had gotten the arm Kira had complained about, saying that there was a birthmark on it that she hadn't liked. I didn't think she'd hated it so much that she'd want a shark to bite it off. I sat down by the bed and looked at her. Reaching out slowly I brushed her hair out of the way as she suddenly popped her eyes open, breathing in deeply like she had been holding her breath for years. Startling me, I jumped and screamed, making Kira turn to me and try to scream. Her voice was hoarse, so it was more of a wheeze, and we looked at each other for the longest time before she relaxed again.

"Am I dead princess," Kira said. She sounded like she hadn't had a drink of water for weeks, and I looked around but couldn't find a glass.

"Shh, don't try and talk, Mama, you're not dead. I'm here now," I said pressing the buzzer for the nurse. Nurses rushed in, and they asked me to leave before they hurriedly closed the curtains and shut the door behind me.

Chapter 11

The next time I saw Kira was two weeks later because I was not immediate family. But I stayed at the hospital for those two weeks, always sitting outside, looking at her through the window when was awake. She had been able to stay awake for long periods at a time, gradually having built that up, and the doctor told me that she should make a full recovery but that he couldn't go into any more detail. I had to start my uni degree in a weeks time, and I was relieved that Kira was allowed to go back home with me at the start of her third week in the hospital.

"It's OK if you don't feel like talking. We don't have to talk," I said driving her home. I had bought a car since I was going to be staying here a while. She just smiled and put her hand on my thigh.

"I hope you don't mind that I'm here. I'll

understand if you want to be alone. And we don't have to worry about our dynamic if it's all just too much," I added, not wanting her to think she had to be something she wasn't ready to be. Kira looked at me with the same amused expression she always had when I began to ramble, and I liked that she hadn't changed that much.

"Princess, everything stays the same. I'm over the moon you are here. I actually don't think I could do this without you, but you might have to help me while I get used to this," Kira said, moving her shoulder. She frowned. The shark had taken her arm up until her mid-upper arm, and I could tell that she could still feel it as though it was there. The doctors had called it 'Phantom feeling,' where she would feel like it was still there even though it wasn't.

"Also, you'll have to get used to me fucking you with this hand," Kira said, laughing. I loved that she could still find humor in this. The shark had taken her writing hand, and I knew she'd be pretty clumsy until she learned how to use her other hand.

"I'm a really good helper, Mama," I said, and I liked that she stroked my hair like she always used to.

"What a bloody awful time for you to come and see me. Did I hear right, you're like staying for school?" Kira asked as we pulled into the hostel. I nodded proudly. I was happy she wanted me here and hadn't pushed me away.

"Clever princess, I expect perfect grades from you, baby," Kira said as we got out of the car and were surrounded by happy backpackers.

The months that followed felt like a blur. I had gone to uni and was doing really well. It helped that I knew what I was doing, but Kira had made me a gold star chart and would frequently tell everyone how clever she thought I was. I had moved in with her in her room, and she had moved the other bunks out so that we had a queen-size bed, a beach rug, and cupboard in the room. It actually looked like a real bedroom, and not a room in the middle of the backpacker hostel. She had been going to therapy and rehab to get used to not having an arm and had made a lot of progress. So much so in fact that she had started saying that it was a waste of time going.

"I just don't think I need to go anymore like going won't bring my arm back, and in fact, I kinda like my new look. I think I rock this," Kira said making me toast for breakfast. She had gotten mad when I hadn't let her do all her usual Mama things for me. She had even slammed some people down when they had criticized me for not doing things like making food and carrying things, thinking that I wasn't being fair to her. I like that she had defended me. I was already trying to work through letting her do her usual stuff for me. I didn't need them, making it any harder.

"I think you should go for like a year, just to give it a really good amount of time before you step away. And maybe don't even step away from all at once, maybe just go less until you don't go at all," I suggested worriedly that going cold turkey on the support front might not be the wisest decision. Kira came out of the kitchen, pushed some empty beer bottles away, and place my eggs and toast in front of me.

"But they are all so whiney! You should hear them," Kira said, stabbing her eggs. I smirked, I hadn't realized she was so independent until the accident.

"Maybe go until the nightmares stop," I said quietly. Kira rolled her eyes.

"That happened for like a week, princess," Kira said more sternly than I would have liked signaling that the conversation was over.

"What are you going to do today?" She said, starting a new topic of discussion. I looked at my watch and was happy it was so early.

"I don't have class until this afternoon, I was hoping that I could come with you guys to fly kites on the beach," I said more asking than telling. Kira nodded.

"Yeah, but I want you to do at least 2 hours study today, you've got that exam that I know you aren't prepared for princess," Kira said. I was happy that it had only been the two of us in the outdoor space of the common area this morning. It made me feel like the backpackers weren't really backpackers, but just our home, and we were just outside. I nodded, finishing my eggs and watching as Kira lay down on the wooden bench we had been sitting at.

"You know, I think tomorrow we should go into town and pick you up a few things, princess," Kira said, closing her eyes, oblivious to Danni, who had come to sit next to me.

"Oh, what kind of things, Kira?!" Danni said making Kira laugh and sit up.

"Wouldn't you like to know!" She replied. All I did was blush and make Danni laugh at me.

"Well, when we all hear sex moans coming from your room, we'll know you have gone shopping," Danni said as she dealt out a hand of cards, starting the day.

"Where's Kira?" I asked, coming home from

class and not having found her in our room. We had all gone kite flying, which had turned into, who could fly a kite blindfolded the longest, who could do it while drinking the longest and who could fly the most kites in one go. I liked that the backpackers always kept life exciting. The class had been easy, and I liked that I knew all the answers. Coming home, I noticed that it had started getting dark earlier and quickly walked past the pub, happy to be almost home.

"I don't know actually, haven't seen her for a few hours, maybe she's gone to get food or something?" Danni suggested. Leaving the common room, I went to our room and had a shower. I hadn't realized that I was so tired, but the minute I lay down on our bed, I was fast asleep.

Waking up, the room was dark, and so was outside. I stretched and looked at the time. It was 1:30 in the morning, and I was surprised I had slept through the party. I could hear going on on the beach. Pulling on some clothes, remembering my jacket, I walked to the beach, thinking that Kira would be there. She loved bonfires and had not missed one since I had known her. I made my way down the beach to the group who were partying and looked for Kira. I walked through the crowd, not catching their excited energy because I felt something else. Something was wrong. I walked to the water's edge, wondering if getting some perspective on the party would make Kira visible. I saw people dancing and drinking, some people sneaking off into the bushes and people just being generally happy to be alive. I turned back around and looked out into the blue and black waves, jumping when I felt her behind me.

"Hey," Kira said, smiling at me. She had wrapped her cardigan around her, and she had looked like she had been crying.

"Hey, what's wrong?" I said, worried that something had happened. Kira just shrugged her shoulders.

"I don't know, wanna walk? I'm not really in the mood to party," Kira said, moving to my other side and taking my hand in hers. I just nodded as she led me away from the warmth of the fire and the loudness of the party. We walked in silence, just feeling the cold night sand under our feet and tasting the salt on our lips. Kira walked slowly in an easy rhythm, and I hoped that she was OK.

"I want to show you," she said quietly as she led me to the jetty. I stopped and pulled on her arm.

"You don't have too if you don't want to, Mama," I said making Kira turn around and smile lovingly at me. She brushed my hair away from my face and kissed me.

"I love that you didn't want to stop being Mama's princess Sasha," Kira said, making me proud to have her love.

"But I want to show you. I need to show you. I think I need to show myself, but I want you here, please princess?" Kira said. It felt strange to have her asking me for permission. I nodded and continued to walk with her to the edge of the jetty.

"This is where it happened," Kira said, looking down into the blackness. I wasn't really sure what I could say so I just held her hand and moved into her lap when she sat down and pulled me to her. She buried her face into my neck and hair, nuzzling me while she played with my tits.

"I hope you are OK with how much I've needed you lately princess, I just really don't think I could do this without you," Kira said, running her fingers over my crossed thighs.

"I'm happy you've still wanted me, I was kinda worried you'd push me away or something," I said as Kira shook her head no.

"No, I could never push you away. You are too precious to me princess," Kira said as I leaned back and melted into her.

"Tell me what happened, Mama," I said softly. Kira patted me tenderly and exhaled like she was trying to rid the memory from her body.

"We were jumping off the end here. I'd gone a couple of times. We were all going to do one last jump. I jumped, but I didn't bother looking down this time. The next thing I know, there's blood everywhere, people are screaming. I didn't feel it at first, the pain, I just looked around wondering what had happened. Then I felt it come back; it hit me on my side and pushed me into the water. I held my breath and shut my eyes," Kira said before becoming silent again. I didn't really know what to say so we stayed sitting in silence, listening to the party going on down the beach watching the ocean glimmer like stars.

Chapter 12

"I've decided I'm going to get it tattooed," Kira said the minute I opened my eyes the next morning. She had obviously been watching me sleep because she was sitting up in bed, looking at me with wide eyes. I blinked a few times and adjusted my ears, getting used to her loud voice so early in the morning.

"What?" I asked, unsure of what she was talking about. Kira rolled her eyes and got up, running to the shelf on the other side of the room.

"Here, this is what I want," she said, handing me a drawing. One of the backpackers had drawn her a mock-up of what her tattoo could look like, and Kira beamed with excitement. It was an image of a big blue-gray shark, surrounded by water but jumping out to bite into the air. It looked cool I had to admit.

"When do you want to get it done?" I asked.

Kira took the drawing from my hands and smiled down at it.

"Soon, princess, right now, let Mama see if you've been a good girl," Kira said feeling the front of my diaper. She frowned and cupped my face making me look at her when I tried to look down.

"You know I don't change you out of your diapy until you've wet it, princess. Mama is going to make breakfast, and when I come back, you'd better have been a good girl for me," Kira said, jumping off the bed and walking out the door. I laid in bed for a minute, thinking of how I could get away with not wetting it, but deciding that was a hopeless case I began as Kira walked back into the room with buttery toast she had just made. She placed the plate down on the table we had set up for eating and came over to feel me.

"Good girl," she said, kissing my forehead.

"I'm pretty sad that I had to ask you to wet your diaper when you know that it's something you have to do. Just because Mama has been a little out of it doesn't mean you can stop being my good little princess Sasha," Kira said taking my hand and making me sit at our table. I hated this. I pouted while I ate my toast, which just made Kira laugh.

"Oh, has the baby forgot who is in charge, little princess?" She said grabbing my cheek and pulling it firmly. I tried to look less pouty, but I was failing. Kira finished her toast before grabbing me by my hair and bending me over her knee.

"I'm not going to spank your ass. I'm going to spank these lovely exposed thighs of yours. Then you can explain to everyone why you are wearing jeans on a hot day like this because, by the time that I am done with you, you'll be red for hours," Kira said, taking a gag and buckling it in place. She had become really good at only using one hand, and I found it so sexy that she could still powerfully dominate me.

"Be quiet, or people might come in here princess, and you know Mama would have no trouble with that," Kira said, making me stop squealing behind my gag. She spanked my thighs, running her nails over the red skin over and over again making me squirm on her lap.

"Hold still, princess I'm not done with you yet," Kira said, spanking me until I felt my legs burn deep in my muscles. I lay there wondering when it would stop when I felt cool balm over my burning skin.

"Pretty princess," Kira said as she made sure my legs would be alright. She turned me over, and I looked at her big brown eyes and found that I was smiling a smile I couldn't wipe from my face.

"Thank you, Mama," I said softly, making her match my smile.

"I won't be bad again," I added, making her laugh.

"Oh, you probably will princess, little girls always say they'll be good but then are naughty," Kira replied standing me up and taking off my diaper. It was late morning, and she let me have a shower and get clean as she picked out what clothes she wanted me in.

"I think you'll be in these and your new

singlet princess," Kira said. The water muffled the sound of her voice, but I knew what she was talking about. I got out of the shower and dried off before walking naked into the room.

"Pretty princess," Kira said, seeing my body and her red handprints on the tops of my thighs.

"Here," Kira plainly said, pointing to the bed. I frowned. We hadn't done this before. She held a pull up, and I wondered what she would do with it.

"You are going to be in this today to remind you of who your Mama is and that you are mine. Lay down," Kira said sliding up my thighs. She slapped my sides, and I lifted my bottom for her as she pulled it on.

"Cute," Kira said, rubbing the front before pulling my jeans up. She bit my nipples, making me giggle and squirm on the bed as she pulled down my singlet, rubbing my nipples under it before putting my paci in my mouth.

"I know you don't have school today, so you'll stay here a while with Mama before we go out this afternoon, princess. Go get your colors and draw Mama a pretty picture," Kira said as I made my way over to my special box of things. Kira had bought me a wooden chest where I could keep my stuffies, coloring in books, pacis, and all my princess things. I liked that it doubled as a table so I could sit on the floor and color until my hands hurt. Kira lay down on the bed and watched me. At first, it always made me so nervous, but as I showed her the bunny I had just drawn and colored and the duck I was working on next, I relaxed as she told me what a clever girl I was.

I felt like Kira knew almost everyone in town, so I wasn't surprised when she had been able to get a tattoo appointment that very afternoon. She had kept me in my little space all day, making me her princess when I tried to be a big girl again. She even held my hand while we walked to the shop even though it was only ten minutes away.

"Hold Mama's hand, little princess," Kira said as we crossed the road. I liked that no one was around us and that we could have our dynamic so open. Kira had told me that we might be there for a few hours and made me pack a juice box and some crackers in my reversible sequin backpack. Kira had bought it for me when she saw how excited I was over my reversible sequin pencil case. I had played for hours with it, making the color change from pink to silver and back again. My backpack was green on one side of the sequins and black on the other, and I loved it.

We walked to the shop, but it looked like it was closed, and I pulled on Kira's arm, worried that she wouldn't be able to get it done.

"It's OK, princess, we aren't going in that way, come on," Kira said going around the back of the shop. It had graffiti on the brick walls and looked scary making me hold her hand tight and snuggle into her.

"Oh little princess, you're alright with Mama," Kira said as the back door was opened for her.

"Hey babe," a burly looking woman said.

She was covered from neck too; I could only imagine, toes in ink. She towered over Kira and made me feel like she was not someone to mess with.

"Hey Star, this is Sasha, my little one I was telling you about," Kira said, making me gasp. *She had told someone about me?!* My head screamed. Star looked at me and smiled sweetly.

"I know someone who is very excited to meet you, little one," Star said leading us into the shop. It was indeed shut, but in the corner, I saw something that blew my mind. Another baby playing with connecting blocks, the small kind. I wondered how 'old' she was. Kira walked me over to her, and I nervously sat down.

"This is Sasha, Evie, she is really excited to play with you," Kira said before kissing me on my cheek and patting my bottom. Kira turned and walked over to where Star was waiting, ready to begin the tattoo. I sat down on the edge of the blanket Evie was sitting on and watched her play for a while before she passed me some blocks.

"You can build the princess tower," Evie said. She was really emo with black hair in high pigtails, a frilly goth style skirt, and I could see she had a thick black diaper on. Her top was a white t-shirt with a big pink skull on the front, and she had suspenders over the top. She had knee-high white socks on, and she giggled when she saw me staring at her.

"Do you think I'm pretty?" Evie asked, making me just shrug my shoulders and nod my head. She had her lip pierced on both sides of her bottom lip and big blue eyes that were lined in heavy eyeliner. She was pretty, but in a kind of way, I never wanted to be.

"You are so quiet," Evie said, taking the tower I offered her after I was finished.

"Oh yeah, Evie, my little princess is shy, sweetie," I heard Kira say. I moved to the corner and watched what was going on. Kira not even grimacing as Star began coloring in her upper arm. Evie was playing mostly by herself and me bringing my knees to my chest and placing my chin on them as I watched. I reached for my backpack and stroked it up and down as I watched. I really just wanted to be by Mama's side but knew that I would just be getting in the way, so I stayed with Evie and took out my crackers and juice.

"Do you want some?" I softly asked Evie, passing her a cracker. She nodded and clapped her hands, eating the cracker in one go and holding out her hand for more. I smiled, and we made a little table out of the blocks and had a picnic. I wasn't sure how much time had passed when Kira came over to where Evie and I were playing and said that we had to go home now. I looked up at her with a slight pouty frown making Star laugh.

"She can stay with us for the night if you'd be happy with that?" She asked Kira. My eyes went wide, and I quickly picked up my backpack and came to cuddle Kira's legs. I liked playing with Evie, but I didn't want to be away for Kira. Kira looked down and stroked my hair.

"I think my little princess is a bit too little for sleepovers just yet. But thanks," she replied. I liked that she always seemed to know how to get out of a situation. Star nodded and reached down to pick up Evie. I was surprised at how strong Star was, and it made me nervous to think of how painful her punishments would be. I could still feel the sting of Kira's hand on me, and she was significantly slimmer and less muscly than Star. After saying goodbye, Kira took my hand and led me back out onto the main street.

"Did you have an OK time princess," Kira asked. Her arm was covered with plastic wrap, and I looked at it curiously when we stopped at the traffic lights.

"You'll see it soon enough, princess. It looks great, though. I'm really happy with it," Kira said.

"Well, that's good Mama because it's permanent," I replied making her laugh.

"Not really, if I don't like it, I'll just get a shark to bite it off or something," Kira said. She held my hand, and for the first time in a long time, I knew that she'd be OK.

"Mama," I said, wondering how I could

bring up the topic I was about to bring up. Kira could tell I was nervous instantly and stopped walking just as we reached the hostel.

"Yeah, princess?" She said, getting comfy on a park bench. The air was still warm even though it was evening, and the crickets chirped in the darkness.

"Tell Mama what's wrong, princess," Kira said lovingly. I looked at her and held her hand.

"I want to move out of there. I want us to get our own place so that we have more room to be like this," I said, making Kira just nod her head slowly.

"But the rent is so cheap, as in, no rent here, princess. Mama can give you so many things because I get the room as part of the job," Kira replied. I just nodded and looked down. I understood why she wanted to stay there, we saved so much money only having to pay my very small amount of rent for water, electricity, and Wi-Fi included, but I wanted to be her baby in more spaces than just a room.

"I think I could arrange something though, princess," Kira said lighting up. She had that wicked gleam in her eye, the same one she had the day I met her, and I held my breath as I waited for her to tell me what her plan was. But Kira just laughed and told me to get ready to have some fun if she pulled it off.

"I've got to run it past a few people first, so I don't want you to get your hopes up, but if I pull this off, I think you'll have a great time!" Kira said leaning forward to kiss me and rub me over my pull up.

Chapter 13

Kira had gone out early the next morning, saying something about needing to use a printer in the backpacker office. I tried to reply, but I was still so asleep I just smiled as she kissed me and rolled back over, never even hearing her close the door behind her.

Getting up a few hours later, Kira had obviously been in and out of the room several times. There were balloons everywhere and colorful bunting, glitter, adult-sized pacifiers, and things to decorate them with.

"Mama?" I said sleepily, looking over at Kira, who was busy tying ribbons onto the balloons. I was excited to see pretty ribbons dangling down from the ceiling.

"Hi sleepy head, did you have a good rest princess?" Kira said, blowing me a kiss.

"Mama, what are you doing?" I asked,

rubbing my eyes and smiled when I saw the big bag of candy Kira had bought.

"Well, you know how you said that you wanted more space to be Mama's little princess in? Well, we are going to have a fundraising party, and all the proceeds are going to go to a charity that looks after sick kids, and everyone has to dress up as a baby, and the winner gets two weeks free rent and a 12 pack of beer," Kira said excitedly without taking a breath. I looked at her in amazement. Seeing my bewilderment, Kira continued.

"There's also going to be competitions for the best coloring in, and the best sandcastle and the best-decorated paci. Here, I made posters," Kira added, handing me a flyer. I had to give it to her, she sure was a clever Mama. I giggled, and she jumped up and cuddled into me on the bed.

"Is Mama the best princess?" Kira asked, tickling me.

"Yes, Mama!" I squealed in happiness that in a few days time, I would have my chance to be little in public.

The hostel was a hive of excitement in the afternoon before the party. I was actually surprised at how into it everyone seemed. Most of the boys had been walking around in just diapers all day, pacifiers strung around their necks, and they looked funny getting day drunk dressed as babies. The girls had taken to it all really well as well, but Danni had decided that she'd rather be a Mommy than a baby and had bought a shirt saying 'Mama bear,' on the front. I was busy putting on my skirt and tucking my shirt into it when Kira came in.

"Princess, let Mama," she said, coming over and helping me.

"Someone looks cute," she said, taking my pacifier and clipping it to my shirt.

"What if they all see that I like it more than just doing it for fun Mama," I softly whispered.

"Oh baby girl, I think you'll find there are a couple of little babies out there that feel the same way. Which is surprising I thought you were the only one here!" Kira said, undressing and pulling on a tight black cotton dress. She took her hair out, and waves of long blonde hair fell down her back, making her look even more beautiful than she already did.

"You don't like them, though, do you, Mama?" I said nervously, not wanting her to fall for someone else. Kira spun around as I had just used a bad word with a horrified look on her face.

"How could you even think that princess?! You are the only little girl I have ever, and will ever want!" Kira said, making my fears instantly disappear. She said I could have my hair down as well, and I liked that it swayed in the breeze. I took a big breathe as I left our room, Kira holding my hand as we walked to the common room. It felt funny to be in a diaper in public like this, but I was happy when no one seemed to care.

Moreover, they seemed jealous of mine. I was wearing a teddy bear print one, and some of the other girls even asked if I had any extras. I giggled as we ran back to mine and Kira's room, and they put them on. I was happy Kira wasn't mad that we were kinda wasting them.

The party started with everyone coloring in trying to have the best picture, Kira running around taking photos and keeping everyone entertained. We all went to the beach and spent hours making huge sandcastles. Some of the guys made a Mommy sandcastle and gave her huge tits, which made everyone laugh. It was such a fun night that I hadn't even realized what time it was by the time people started passing out on the beach or in the common room. I had been busy decorating a new paci with some of the other girls when I felt Kira come up behind me and playing with my hair.

"Wow, amazing skills, you have little ones," Kira teased, but I knew she wasn't really teasing.

"Time for bed, though, I've got to lock up the room now," she added, taking my hand and lifting up my arm, making me stand. The other girls stacked their chairs loudly, making the three guys who had passed out on the couches wake up and slowly make their way back to their rooms.

"That was the best night ever, Mama!" I exclaimed as soon as we walked into our room. Kira smiled and picked a leaf out of my hair.

"I'm so happy you had fun, baby. Mama did good," Kira said reaching into the shower and turning it on.

"Shower and beddys baby girl," Kira added, taking off my clothes and diaper. She had changed me twice during the night as I wet my diaper, not being able to hold all the drinks we were consuming. I knew that the moment I lay in bed, I would be asleep, and I guess Kira knew that too because as I dried myself off, she pulled a pull up on me quick and didn't bother dressing me in anything else as she tucked me into bed.

"Sweet dreams, little princess, Mama loves you," Kira said kissing my forehead as I fell asleep, holding onto her finger.

Who is Tina Moore?

Tina Moore has enjoyed the lifestyle of a Mommy Domme for several years. She began exploring kink and BDSM in her youth and found her love of being a strict Mommy Domme in early 2000. Tina Moore is now an author of many MDLG and ABDL themed novels.

Having enjoyed many years in the kink community, Tina Moore combines these experiences with the sweet and naughty things her baby girl does to bring you tantalizing and salacious stories.

Follow her on:

Author Page on Amazon

Instagram @tinamoore.kdp